THE TIME MACHINE

H.G. WELLS

CONDENSED AND ADAPTED BY
W.T. ROBINSON

ILLUSTRATED BY
JASON ALEXANDER

Dalmatian 🐾 Press™

The Dalmatian Press Children's Classics Collection
has been adapted and illustrated with care and thought,
to introduce you to a world of famous authors, characters, ideas,
and great stories that have been loved for generations.

Editor — Kathryn Knight
Creative Director — Gina Rhodes
And the entire classics project team of Dalmatian Press

ALL ART AND EDITORIAL MATERIAL OWNED BY DALMATIAN PRESS, LLC

ISBN: 1-57759-539-4 mass
1-57759-565-3 base

First Published in the United States in 2001 by Dalmatian Press, LLC, USA

Copyright©2001 Dalmatian Press, LLC

Printed and bound in the U.S.A.

The DALMATIAN PRESS name and spotted spine logo are
trademarks of Dalmatian Press, LLC, Franklin, Tennessee 37067.

11435

02 03 04 LBM 10 9 8 7 6 5 4 3

A note to the reader—

A classic story rests in your hands. The characters are famous. The tale is timeless.

Although this is not the original version (which you really *must* read when you're ready for every detail), this Dalmatian Press Children's Classic has been shortened and adapted especially for you. We kept the well-known phrases for you. We kept the author's style. And we kept the important imagery and heart of the tale.

Literature is terrific fun! It encourages you to think. It helps you dream. It is full of heroes and villains, suspense and humor, adventure and wonder, and new ideas. It introduces you to writers who reach out across time to say: "Do you want to hear a story I wrote?"

Curl up and enjoy.

DALMATIAN PRESS
ILLUSTRATED CLASSICS

CONTENTS

CHARACTERS

TIME TRAVELER — a clever, inventive man who tells an amazing story to his dinner guests

NARRATOR — the dinner guest who has written this tale down for us

DOCTOR — a guest who thinks the Time Traveler is full of clever tricks

PSYCHOLOGIST — a guest who thinks the Time Traveler is full of wild ideas

FILBY — a red-haired man who likes to argue

YOUNG MAN — a guest with some good ideas about how to use "time traveling"

TOWN MAYOR — yet another doubting guest

CHARACTERS

EDITOR — a newspaper editor, named
Mr. Blank, who likes to speak in "headlines"

JOURNALIST — a newspaper writer, named
Mr. Dash, who is a friend of the Editor

SILENT MAN — a guest named Mr. Chose
who chooses not to say a word at dinner

MRS. WATCHETT — the housekeeper at the
Time Traveler's home

ELOI — the sweet, calm little people of the
future who live with no cares... or do they?

MORLOCKS — the creatures who live down in
the horrible, grinding wells, and who *also* enjoy
having dinner guests...

THE
TIME MACHINE

CHAPTER ONE

The Time Traveler's New Idea

The Time Traveler (which is what we now call him) was trying to explain one of his strange new ideas to us. Our usual Thursday evening dinner party at his home was about to become… unusual.

There were six of us at his home. The Doctor, the Town Mayor, the Psychologist, a Young Man (whom I did not know), Filby, and of course myself.

Supper was over, and we went into the library. The fire burned brightly. Its light made the bubbles in our drinking glasses sparkle. We all sat in comfortable chairs that *he* had made (for he was a very clever man). His gray eyes shone and twinkled, full of excitement as he spoke.

"You must listen carefully," he said. "You might not understand some of the things I'm going to tell you. For instance, some of the math they taught you in school is wrong."

"Do you expect us to believe that?" said Filby, a red-haired man who liked to argue.

"Give me a moment. Then, I think you will agree with me. Your math teachers taught you that you could only measure something in three ways—we measure its Length, Width, and Height. Am I right?"

"That is right, but what is your point?" said the Psychologist.

"My point is this. I am quite sure that a thing can be measured in *four* ways. And the fourth way I am talking about is measuring *where* it is—in Time. The only difference between Time and the other three measurements is that Time is not something we can touch. Time is just in our minds. Do you follow me?"

"That," said the Young Man, "is not very clear."

"*I* have never heard of any Four-Way-Measuring mathematics, or whatever you call it," said the Town Mayor.

"Well," said the Time Traveler, "I do not mind telling you that I have been at work on this puzzle for a long time. The more I have thought about it, the more certain I am that I am right. We can move in four directions to measure an object. Along its width. Along its length. Along its height. And… along its place in Time."

"But," said the Doctor, staring hard at a coal in the fire, "if Time is really only a fourth dimension, why can't we move in Time just as we move around in the other directions—left and right, up and down…?"

"Ah, but until man invented hot air balloons, could we really move up and down as we wished? No. We needed a machine to go against the force of gravity. Well, I have invented something, too. Something that will let us move around in Time."

"But you cannot get away from this very minute or this very day," said the Doctor.

"My dear sir, that is just where you are wrong. We are *always* getting away from the here and now. Don't you ever think about tomorrow or yesterday? Our minds are really traveling in Time, yes?"

"But that is only in our mind," said the Psychologist. "We're talking about moving from one place to another. You cannot move from one place to another in *Time*."

"Are you sure? Let me try again. As I've said, if I am thinking about something, I can go back and remember it very clearly. I can go to the very instant something happened in my mind. I jump back for a moment. Up to now we haven't known of a way to stay there, any more than an animal could figure out how to stay up in the air in a balloon. But man is smarter than an animal. So why can't he figure out a way to travel backward or forward in Time just as we travel back and forth and up and down? If our minds can move in Time, *we* can, too. All we need is the right math and the right invention."

"Oh, *this*," began Filby, "is too silly to believe."

"Why?" said the Time Traveler.

"It makes no sense," said Filby.

"What do you mean?" said the Time Traveler.

"You can tell me something with clever words," said Filby, "but that doesn't make it true. You will never make me believe it."

"Maybe not," said the Time Traveler. "But now you begin to see the point of my studies of Time. Long ago I had an idea for a machine—"

"A machine that could travel through Time?" exclaimed the Young Man.

"Yes, one that would travel in any direction in both Space and Time. The driver of my machine could ride right along with it into the future or the past."

Filby just laughed.

"But I have proof! I can even show you an experiment," said the Time Traveler.

"It *would* be very useful for studying history," the Psychologist said. "We could travel back and see how the whale swallowed Jonah!"

"And how about going into the future?" added the Young Man. "Just think! You could travel forward in time, watch a horse race, and then come back in time and make a bet on the winning horse!"

"You might even find new ways of life or new kinds of people," added the Time Traveler.

"Of all the wild ideas!" began the Psychologist.

"Yes, that's what I thought. That's why I never talked much about it until now," said the Time Traveler.

"Proof!" I shouted. "You said you had proof!"

"And you said something about an experiment!" cried Filby, whose brain was getting tired of all this.

"Yes, let us see your experiment," said the Psychologist. "But it's all foolishness, you know."

The Time Traveler smiled at us as he walked slowly out of the room. We heard his slippers shuffling down the long hall to his workshop.

The Psychologist looked at us. "I wonder what he's got?"

"Oh, a clever trick of some kind," said the Doctor.

CHAPTER TWO

A Clever Trick of Some Kind

When the Time Traveler came back into the room, he was carrying a strange machine. It had a glittering metal frame, not much larger than a small clock. There was ivory in it, and something that looked like crystal. What happened next is hard to describe—and even harder to believe.

He set a small table in front of the fireplace. Then he placed a small lamp on the table along with the little machine. He pulled up a chair and sat down. We all gathered around the Time Traveler, watching him closely. The room was well lighted, and I didn't see how he could play a trick on us.

The Time Traveler looked at us. Then he looked at the machine.

"Well?" said the Psychologist.

"This little box," said the Time Traveler, "is only a model. It is much smaller than the one that will carry a man through time. You will see that there is an odd twinkling look about this bar." He pointed to the bar with his finger. "Also, here is one little white lever, and here is another."

The Doctor got up and looked into the thing. "It's beautifully made," he said.

"It took me two years to make," said the Time Traveler.

We all had a careful look at the machine.

"Now I want you to understand that pressing this lever sends the machine into the future," he went on. "This other one sends it into the past. This saddle is the seat of a time traveler. Shortly, I am going to press a lever, and off the machine will go. It will pass into Time and disappear. Have a good look at the thing. Look at the table, too, to be sure there is no trick. I don't want to waste this model and then be told I was a quack."

For a short time, things were quiet. Then the Time Traveler moved his finger toward the lever.

"No," he said suddenly. "Give me your hand." He turned to the Psychologist and took his hand. Then he told him to push a lever. So it was the Psychologist himself who sent the model Time Machine on its endless journey.

We all saw the lever turn. I am certain there was no trick. There was a rush of wind. One of the candles was blown out, and the little machine suddenly began spinning and became a blur. It looked like a sparkling ghost of brass and ivory. Then it was gone—disappeared! The table was empty except for the small lamp.

Everyone was silent for a minute. Then Filby said he had never seen anything like it.

The Psychologist came out of his daze and began looking under the table.

The Time Traveler laughed cheerfully.

"Well?" He smiled, for he knew that the Psychologist had found nothing.

We stared at each other.

"Look here," said the Doctor, "are you serious about this? Do you really believe that machine has traveled into Time?"

"Certainly," said the Time Traveler, going over to stir the fire. "Furthermore, I have a big machine

nearly finished in there—" (he pointed toward the workshop) "—and when that is ready, I plan to take a trip of my own."

"You mean to say that the model has traveled into the future?" said Filby.

"Into the future or the past—I don't actually know for sure. What do think about all this now?"

"It sounds believable enough tonight," said the Doctor, "but wait until tomorrow. Wait for the clear, common sense of the morning."

"Would you like to see the real Time Machine?" asked the Time Traveler. And, taking the lamp in his hand, he led the way down the hall to his workshop. I remember the flickering light and the dance of the shadows. We all followed him, puzzled.

When we got to the workshop we saw another machine, just like the toy model we had seen disappear before our eyes, only much larger. Parts were of nickel, parts of ivory, and parts had been cut out of crystal. There were some unfinished bars on a bench. I picked one up to have a better look at it. It seemed to be made of quartz.

"Look here," said the Doctor, "*are* you serious, or is this some kind of trick?"

"Upon that machine," said the Time Traveler, holding the lamp up, "I am going to explore Time. Is that clear? I have never been more serious in my life."

None of us knew quite how to take it.

I caught Filby's eye. He winked at me.

CHAPTER THREE

In Time, Our Host Arrives

At that time none of us quite believed in the Time Machine. The Time Traveler was a very clever man, and we weren't sure we could trust him. We always suspected some surprise or trick hiding behind his strange ideas.

The next Thursday I went again to the Time Traveler's home for dinner. I arrived late and found four or five men already there. The Doctor was standing in front of the fireplace with a sheet of paper in one hand and his pocket watch in the other. I looked around for the Time Traveler.

"It's half-past seven now," said the Doctor. "I suppose we'd better have dinner."

"Where's the Time Traveler?" I asked, taking my seat at the table.

"It's rather odd," said the Doctor. "He'll be a little late. He asks me in this note to go ahead with dinner if he's not back. He says he'll explain things when he comes. He's already a half-hour late."

"It seems a shame to let the dinner get cold," said the Editor of a well-known daily newspaper. The rest of us agreed, and the Doctor rang the bell for the servants.

I looked around at the group. The Psychologist was the only person besides the Doctor and myself who had been at last week's dinner. Mr. Blank the Editor was there. I also saw Mr. Dash the Journalist, and another man—a silent, shy fellow with a beard—whom I didn't know. This Silent Man, whose name was Mr. Chose, never said a thing all evening.

There was talk at the dinner table about why the Time Traveler might be missing. I said he might be Time Traveling. The Editor asked what I meant by this, and the Psychologist and I gave him the whole story of what we had seen the week before.

Then, without a sound, the door from the hall opened slowly. I was facing the door.

"Hello!" I said. "At last!"

The door opened a bit more and the Time Traveler stood before us.

The Doctor saw him next. "Good heavens, man! What's the matter?" he cried.

Everyone at the table turned toward the door.

He was in sad shape. He looked tired and thin, as if he had suffered a great amount. His coat was dusty and dirty and smeared with green down the sleeves. His hair was a wild tangle, and seemed to me to be grayer—either with dust and dirt, or because its color had really changed. His face was horribly pale. His chin had a brown cut on it—not yet healed.

For a moment he stayed in the doorway, as if the light had dazed him. Then he came into the room, walking with a bad limp. We watched him in silence, expecting him to speak. He said not a word, but came painfully toward the table.

"What on earth have you been doing, man?" said the Doctor.

The Time Traveler did not seem to hear. "Don't let me disturb you," he said, a bit weakly. "I'm all right." He looked into our faces for a moment. Then he spoke again, still a little unsure of his words.

"I'm feeling a bit strange. I'll be all right in a minute. I'm going to wash and dress, and then I'll come down and explain things… Save me some of that meat. I'm starving for a bit of meat."

He turned and walked toward the stairway door. Again I noticed his limp and the soft padding sound of his footsteps. I saw that he had nothing on his feet but soiled and torn bloodstained socks. The door closed behind him.

For a minute, my mind was daydreaming. Then I heard the Editor say, "REMARKABLE BEHAVIOR OF A FAMOUS SCIENTIST." (The newspaper Editor liked to speak in "headlines.") This brought my attention back to the bright dinner table.

"What's going on here?" said the Journalist.

I looked at the Psychologist, who seemed to be thinking what I was thinking. I thought of the Time Traveler's limp as he went painfully upstairs. I don't think anyone else had noticed this.

All of the dinner talk soon turned to time traveling and the Time Traveler's strange machine. The guests who had not been at last Thursday's dinner could not believe what they heard. The Editor asked, "What *is* this time traveling? A man couldn't cover himself with dust by rolling around

in a metal machine, could he? Ah! There must not be any clothes-brushes in the Future," he joked.

When the Time Traveler came back he was dressed in clean clothes, but his face still looked tired and worn out.

"I say," said the Editor with great laughter, "these fellows tell me you have been traveling into the middle of next week!"

The Time Traveler came to his place at the table without a word. He smiled quietly, in his old way.

"There must be a story for the newspaper here!" cried the Editor. "I want the story!"

"Never mind the story!" said the Time Traveler. "I want something to eat. I won't say a word until I get some meat into my body. Thanks. And please pass the salt."

"Give us at least *one* word," I said. "Have you been time traveling?"

"Yes," said the Time Traveler, with his mouth full, nodding his head.

"I'd give good money for the full story," said the Editor eagerly.

The Time Traveler said nothing. The rest of the dinner was uncomfortable. Questions kept coming to my mind. The Journalist tried to make jokes.

The Silent Man seemed nervous. And the Time Traveler only seemed interested in his dinner. He ate like a tramp who hadn't had a good meal in a long time. The Doctor watched the Time Traveler out of the side of his eye. At last, the Time Traveler pushed his plate away and looked at us.

"I was starving. I've had a most incredible time. But let's go into the library. It's too long a story to tell over dirty plates." He rang the bell for the servants. Then he led the way into the library.

"Have you told our new guests about the Time Machine?" he asked me, leaning back in his chair.

"Yes, he has, but the whole thing is foolishness and nonsense," said the Editor.

"I can't argue tonight," said the Time Traveler. "I don't mind telling you the story, but I'm too weak to argue. I will tell you everything that has happened to me—I want to tell you—but you must not interrupt. Most of it will sound like lying. But it's true—every word of it. I was in my workshop at three o'clock, and since then … I've lived eight days … such days as no human being ever lived before! I'm nearly worn out, but I shall not sleep until I've told this whole story. Then I shall go to bed. But no stopping me in the middle! Do you agree to that?"

"Agreed," said the Editor.

The rest of us echoed, "Agreed."

And with that, the Time Traveler began his strange story.

I will now write the story as best I can recall. You will find it amazing, though you cannot hear his voice. And you cannot imagine what it was like to see the Time Traveler's face as he told this story—white and honest, in the bright circle of the little lamp.

At first we all looked back and forth at each other.

After a while, we looked only at the Time Traveler's face.

CHAPTER FOUR

The Flight Through Time

"I told some of you last Thursday about the Time Machine. It's back there in the workshop now—a little wrecked from the trip. One of the ivory bars is cracked, and a brass rail is bent, but the rest of it is in pretty good condition.

"I had to have a new nickel bar remade for it yesterday, but I finally finished building. At ten o'clock this morning, the first of all Time Machines began its career. I gave it a last tap. I tried all the screws again and applied one more drop of oil. Then I sat myself in the saddle. I had no idea what would come next. I had a fear and wonder of the unknown.

"I took the starting lever in one hand and the stopping lever in the other. I pressed the starting one, and almost instantly the stopping one. I seemed to wobble and shake. Then I felt as if I were falling, like in a nightmare. Looking around, I saw the workshop exactly as it had looked before. Had anything happened? For a moment I thought that my mind had tricked me. Then I noticed the clock. A moment before, or so it seemed, it had read a minute or so past ten. Now it was nearly half-past three!

"My little test run had gone all right. So, I took a breath, set my teeth, grabbed the starting lever with both hands, and went off with a bang. The workshop got hazy and went dark. I saw my housekeeper, Mrs. Watchett, come in. She walked, as if she could not see me, toward the garden door. I suppose it took her a minute or so, but to me she seemed to shoot across the room like a rocket. I pressed the lever over to its full-speed position. The night came as fast as turning out a lamp. And in another moment, tomorrow came. My entire workshop grew hazier and hazier. Night came black—then day again—night again—day again—faster and faster still. A buzz filled my ears.

"I am afraid I cannot describe the weird feelings of time traveling. They are very unpleasant. There is a feeling of helpless, forward tumbling! I also felt as if any second there would be a horrible smash. As I put on more speed, night followed day like the flapping of a black wing. My workshop was now just a faint memory. I saw the sun hopping swiftly across the sky. Every minute a whole day went by. I was already going too fast to see any moving things. Even the slowest snail that ever crawled would have dashed by too fast for me to see.

"The blinking dark and light was painful to my eyes. In the times of darkness, I saw the moon spinning swiftly through all of its phases, from new to full.

"As I went on, still gaining speed, the changes from night to day turned into a gray fog. The sky became a wonderful deep blue, the color of early twilight.

"The sun became a streak of fire. In space, the moon was a fainter, flickering ribbon.

"I could see nothing of the stars, except now and then a brighter circle twinkling in the blue.

"I saw
trees growing
and changing like
puffs of mist— first green,
then brown, then shriveled and dead.
I saw huge buildings rise up, then pass like
dreams. The whole surface of the earth seemed
changed. It melted and flowed before my eyes.

"The little hands on the speed dials swung around faster and faster. I was traveling at over a year per minute.

"Minute by minute, winter snow flashed across the world and disappeared, followed right behind by the bright, brief green of spring.

"My fear turned into a wild excitement. The machine started to sway, but my mind was too mixed up to worry about it. So, with a kind of crazy madness, I threw myself into the future. At first I hardly thought of stopping, hardly thought of anything but these new sights and feelings. But soon, some ideas filled my mind.

"I began to wonder: what would this future world be like? What wonderful new changes might there be? I began to see great, beautiful buildings rising around me, larger than any buildings of our own time. I saw a richer green on the hillside. It stayed there, without ever turning to winter. Even in my confusion, the earth seemed very pleasant. And so, I began to think about stopping.

"But then I worried that I would crash into something when I stopped. As long as I was moving at high speed through Time, I was slipping like a mist through everything. But I had no idea what would happen when I slowed down. Then I grew angry over my lack of courage. Like an impatient fool, I pulled the stopping lever. The machine went tumbling out of control, and I was tossed headfirst through the air.

"There was a crashing sound of thunder. A stinging hail was hissing around me. The machine was upside down and I was sitting on soft grass in front of it. I was on what looked like a little lawn in a garden, with azalea bushes everywhere. I noticed that their purple blossoms were dropping in the shower of hailstones. The bouncing, dancing hail hung in a cloud over the machine and rolled along the ground like smoke. I was soon wet to the skin.

"I thought what a fool I was to get wet. I stood up for a better look around. A huge figure carved out of a white stone appeared through the storm, out beyond the bushes. Everything else of the world was hidden.

"As the sheets of hail grew thinner, I saw the white figure more clearly. It was very large, for a silver birch tree touched its shoulder. It was of white marble, shaped like a Sphinx with wings. The base on which it sat appeared to be made of ancient bronze, coated over with a thick, green crust. The eyes of the White Sphinx seemed to watch me. There was the faint shadow of a smile on its lips. At last, I tore my eyes from it and saw that the sky was getting brighter. The sun was peeking through the clouds.

"I looked up again at the crouching white shape, and my fear came back. What might appear when I could see more clearly? What might have happened to human beings? What if the people here thought cruelty was more important than kindness? I might seem like some savage old-world animal to them. My life could be in danger.

"Now I began to see other large shapes. I saw huge buildings with tall pillars. I saw a wooded hillside dimly coming into view as the storm let up. I became more afraid and turned quickly to the Time Machine, trying hard to set it upright. As I did, the rays of the sun broke through the thunderstorm. The gray rain was swept aside. A blue summer sky appeared. The great buildings stood out clearly, shining with the wet of the rain, and covered in white, unmelted hailstones.

"I felt all alone in a strange world. I felt as a small bird might feel who knows the hawk waits above to attack. My fear grew to panic. I took a deep breath, set my teeth, and again wrestled with the machine. Finally, it turned over. With one hand on the saddle and the other on the lever, I stood breathing hard, ready to climb on again and get away from there.

"But in a few moments, my courage returned. I became more curious and less afraid of this world of the distant future. I looked around again.

"In a round opening high up in the wall of a building, I saw a group of figures dressed in rich, soft robes. They had seen me, and they were looking at me.

CHAPTER FIVE

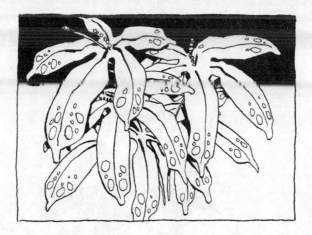

The People of the Future

"I heard voices coming near me. Men were running through the bushes by the White Sphinx. One came down a small path that led straight to the little lawn where I stood with my machine. He was a small creature—perhaps four feet tall—dressed in a purple robe tied at the waist with a leather belt. He had a beautiful and graceful face, and he looked frail and weak. When I saw him, I instantly felt less afraid. I took my hands from the Time Machine.

"In another moment we were standing face to face. He came straight up to me and laughed into my eyes. I saw that he showed no sign of fear.

"He turned to the two others who were following him and spoke to them in a strange language.

"There were more coming, and before long, a little group of perhaps eight or ten of these pretty creatures were around me. One of them spoke to me. I wondered if my voice would be too deep or hard for him, so I did not speak. Instead I made signs to show I did not understand. He came a step forward, waited, and touched my hand. Then I felt other soft little touches on my back and shoulders. They wanted to make sure I was real. This was not at all frightening to me. There was something in these pretty little people that gave me confidence. They were graceful, childlike, and gentle. And besides, they looked so weak that I knew I could throw a whole dozen of them around like bowling pins if I had to.

"I saw their little pink hands feeling at the Time Machine, so I made a sudden move to warn them. Then, before it was too late, I thought of something I had forgotten to do. I reached over the bars of the Time Machine, unscrewed the two levers and put them in my pocket. Then I turned again to see if I could find a way to talk to the little people.

"At the same time I saw some more strange things about them. They looked like pretty dolls. Their curly hair ended at the neck and cheek. There was not a bit of hair on their faces, and their ears were tiny. The mouths were small, with bright red, thin lips, and the little chins were pointed. The eyes were large and calm.

"They made no effort to speak with me, but simply stood around smiling and making soft cooing sounds to each other. I began the conversation. I pointed to the Time Machine and to myself. Then, thinking for a moment how to explain Time, I pointed to the sun. At once, a strangely pretty little figure in purple and white clothing amazed me by making a sound like thunder.

"For a moment I was shocked by this simple response. Were these creatures fools? You see, I had always thought that the people hundreds of thousands of years into the future would be way ahead of us in knowledge, art—everything. Yet one of them had asked me a question, in his own way, that one of our five-year-old children might ask. He had asked me, in fact, if I had come from the sun in a thunderstorm!

"I was disappointed. I had hoped the little bodies and simple clothing had not meant these little people also had simple minds. What good was it to travel into the year 802,701 A.D. and find *less* intelligence? (I should explain that 802,701 A.D. was the exact reading on the dials of my machine.) For a moment I felt that my Time Machine had been a waste of time.

"I nodded to the creatures, pointed to the sun, and made the sound of loud thunder. They all backed away a step or so and bowed. Then one came toward me, laughing and carrying a necklace of beautiful flowers which he put around my neck. The flowers were a kind I had never seen before. You cannot imagine what wonderful flowers had been created over the thousands of years. All the little people laughed and clapped and ran in circles, throwing flowers on me until I was almost covered with them. Then someone made a kind of sign that their plaything (me!) should be put on display in the nearest building. They led me past the Sphinx of white marble, which still seemed to be smiling at me all this time, toward a large gray building. I left the Time Machine sitting by itself on the grass.

"Just inside the doors of the building was a large hall. The floor was made of huge blocks of some very hard, white metal. It was worn down into paths where many feet had walked back and forth for thousands of years. There were many tables made of blocks of polished stone raised about a foot off the floor. On the tables were fruits of all kinds. Some looked like overgrown raspberries and oranges, but most of them I had never seen before.

"We all sat down on cushions on the floor. They began to eat the fruit with their hands, tossing peels into round openings in the sides of the tables. I joined right in with them, for I felt thirsty and hungry. As I did so, I looked around the huge room.

"The first thing I noticed was how old and run-down it was. The windows were broken in many places, and the curtains were thick with dust. But everything about the room still looked rich and beautiful. There were at least two hundred people eating in the hall. Most of them were watching me, their little eyes shining over the fruit they were eating. All were dressed in the same soft, silky clothes.

"Fruit was the only thing they ate. And while I was with them, although I would have loved some meat, I had to eat fruit also. I found out later that horses, cattle, sheep, dogs, and even reptiles had disappeared over time. But the fruits tasted good and I was hungry.

CHAPTER SIX

First Lessons—First Ideas

"As soon as my stomach was full, I decided that the next thing I should do was learn some of the speech of these new people. The names of their fruits seemed a good thing to begin with. Holding one of these up, I began to make sounds and signs. I had a hard time making them understand that I wanted to know its name. At first they just laughed at me, but after a short time a pretty little creature seemed to get my meaning and repeated a name. They chattered back and forth to each other, and I felt like a school teacher among children. At times they were quite amused with the way I pronounced their words.

"Before long, I had learned at least twenty or thirty words. But it was slow work, and the little people soon got tired and wanted to get away from my questions. I realized I'd have to make the lessons shorter. It wasn't long before they had all wandered off to do other things, and I was left alone. I decided to look around outside some more.

"The evening was calm and quiet as I came out of the great hall, and everything was lit by the warm glow of the setting sun. At first, things were very confusing. Everything was so different from the world I had known—not just the foods and flowers. I decided to climb to the top of a small hill where I could get a better view of the world in this year of 802,701 A.D.

"As I walked, I looked for any clue that might help me understand this world I was in. It seemed to be filled with old ruins of things once wonderful and grand. A little way up the hill, for instance, was a great pile of granite stone fastened together with aluminum. It was the crumbling remains of some huge building. But what it had been used for, I could not tell. Later, a very strange thing happened to me here. You will learn about that as my story goes on.

"And then I had another thought. I looked at the half-dozen little people that were following me. I saw that they all had the same kind of costume, the same soft, hairless faces. They all seemed delicate and calm—the women and the men and the children. When I saw the comfort and peace in which these people lived, I thought that maybe there was no more violence or fear in this future world. Maybe it was one big happy family.

"I found out later I was wrong about this. There was an ugly side to this new world. I just hadn't seen it yet.

"While I was thinking about these things, I saw something that caught my attention. It was a pretty structure that looked like a water well with a covering over it. I thought it strange that there were still wells this far in the future. It seemed to me that these people would long ago have invented central water systems. The thought left me, and I walked on.

"I was all alone now. The little legs following me had not been able to keep up. With a strange sense of freedom and adventure, I pushed on up to the very top of the hill.

"There, I found a seat of some yellow metal that I had never seen before. It was covered in places with a pink rust and in other places by soft moss. The armrests were shaped to look like griffins. I sat down on it and looked out across our old world under the sunset of that long day. It was as nice a sight as I have ever seen. The sky was a flaming gold, touched with streaks of purple and red. There were no hedges or fences. The whole earth had become one big garden that belonged to everybody. Was there was any danger in this beautiful land? Perhaps there was. But, for now, everything was peaceful and green.

"There were no bugs in the air and no weeds in the earth. Everywhere were fruits and sweet, delightful flowers. Colorful butterflies flew here and there. There seemed to be no sickness among the people.

"There had been other changes, too—changes in the ways people lived, worked, and got along together. I saw people living in beautiful buildings, dressed in beautiful clothes, doing no work. There were no signs of fights over money or power. No shops or factories. It seemed to me on that golden evening that I had found paradise.

"I thought I had figured out this new world with these sweet little people. My ideas about them seemed simple and easy enough—as most *wrong* ideas are! For, as you know, you cannot know what's inside a book just by looking at its cover. And, as you shall see, there was a lot more to this future earth than what could be seen on its surface.

CHAPTER SEVEN

The Time Machine is Missing!

"As I stood there in the fading twilight, the full moon came up with a silver glow. The little figures stopped moving around below. An owl flew by, and I shivered with the cool of the night. I decided to go down the hill and find a place where I could sleep.

"I looked for the building I had seen before. Then my eye moved to the figure of the White Sphinx. It became clearer as the light of the rising moon grew brighter. I could see the silver birch tree against it. There was the tangle of azalea bushes, and there was the little lawn. I looked at the lawn again. 'No,' I said to myself, 'that *couldn't* be the lawn. I see no Time Machine sitting there.'

"But it *was* the lawn—for the white face of the Sphinx was facing it. All at once I knew the awful truth—the Time Machine was gone!

"The thought of being left helpless in this strange new world came like a slap across the face. I could feel fear grab me by the throat and stop my breathing. Without the Time Machine I could never return to my own time—and my own home!

"In another second I was running with great leaps down the hill. Once, I fell headfirst and cut my face. I jumped up and ran on, warm blood running down my cheek and chin. My breath came with pain. I hated myself for not staying with the machine. I cried out, but nobody answered. Not a creature seemed to be moving in the moonlight.

"When I reached the lawn, my fears came true. The Time Machine was nowhere around. I felt faint and cold when I looked at the empty space where it had been. I ran around, hoping to find it hidden in a corner. Then I stopped still, with my hands clutching my hair.

"There was the huge Sphinx, white, shining, scaly, in the light of the moon. Only the Sphinx. It seemed to smile at my fear.

"For a minute, I hoped the little people might have put the machine away somewhere for me. But I knew they were not strong enough to move it. That is what really scared me. There must be some other stronger creature that I hadn't seen yet. At least I knew the machine could not have moved in Time, because I had the starting levers in my pocket. So it must be hidden somewhere here in this part of the Future. But where could it be?

"I think I must have gone a bit crazy. I remember running in and out among the bushes and scaring some white animal that I thought was a small deer. I beat the bushes with my fist until my knuckles were cut and bleeding. Then, sobbing from my mental pain, I went down to the great building of stone. The big hall was dark, silent, and empty. I slipped on the uneven floor and fell over one of the tables, almost breaking my leg. I lit a match and went on past the dusty curtains, which I have already told you about.

"There I found another big room where twenty or more of the little people were sleeping. I am sure they thought I was strange as I came suddenly out of the quiet darkness with weird noises and a flaming match, for they knew nothing of matches.

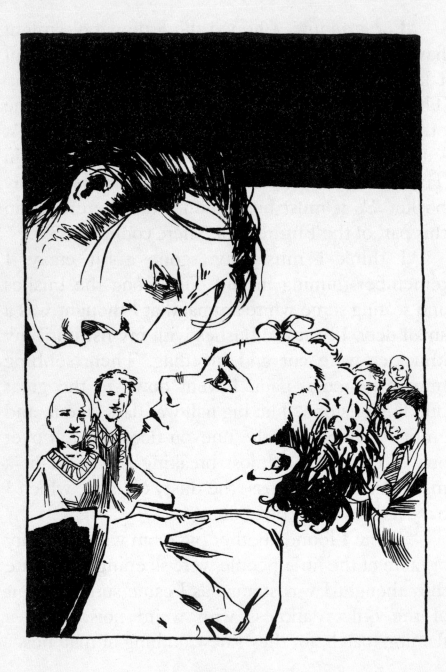

" 'Where is my Time Machine?' I yelled, like an angry child, grabbing them and shaking them. Some laughed at me. It came to me that I was doing a foolish thing by trying to make them afraid of me. For, from what I had seen of them earlier, I thought humans had long ago forgotten what fear was.

"I threw down the match and knocked over one of the people in my path. I went blundering across the big dining hall again, out under the moonlight. I do not remember all I did as the moon crept up the sky.

"Losing my Time Machine made me almost lose my mind. I remember looking everywhere and touching strange creatures in the black shadows. I lay down on the ground near the Sphinx and cried. I had nothing left but sadness.

"Then I slept, and when I awoke it was daytime. A couple of sparrows were hopping around me on the grass.

"I scrambled to my feet and looked around, wondering where I could take a bath. I felt tired, stiff, and dirty. I wanted to feel as fresh as the morning air. But I could not get the loss of the Time Machine off my mind.

"I wasted some time trying to get the little people to understand my questions of them. They could not get any meaning from my signs. The ground of the little lawn gave me some better clues. I found a path ripped in the grass, about halfway between the Sphinx and the spot where my machine had been. There were also signs of strange footprints which led me to the base of the Sphinx. I tapped on it. It sounded hollow. I knew then that my Time Machine was inside. How it got there I did not know.

"I saw the heads of two people in orange clothing coming toward me through the bushes and under some blossom-covered apple trees. I smiled and waved to them. Then, pointing to the White Sphinx, I tried to tell them I wanted to get inside the base on which it sat. The little people just walked away. They had no idea what I was trying to say.

"But I did not give up. I banged with my fist at the bronze doors. I thought I heard something laughing inside, but I wasn't sure. I got a rock from the river and hammered on the doors, but nothing happened. I sat down on the grass to rest for a little while.

"After my short rest I got up and began walking through the bushes toward the hill again.

" 'Take your time,' I said to myself.

"Then I began smiling. I thought of all those years I had spent in study and work to get into the Future… and now, here I was trying to get out of it.

"I couldn't help laughing out loud at myself.

CHAPTER EIGHT

Little Weena

"Over the next day or two I learned to speak a few more words in the language of the little people. I also kept searching here and there for signs of my Time Machine.

"As I looked around I saw more of those strange, covered wells. Several seemed to me to be very deep. One was near the path up the hill which I had followed during my first walk. I sat on the edge of this one and looked down into the dark, gray hole. I could see no sign of water, but I heard a strange sound—a thud-thud-thud, like the beating of some big engine. It was very mysterious. Was there something living under the ground?

"And what about the Time Machine? Something, I didn't know what, had taken it into the hollow base of the White Sphinx. Why? For the life of me I could not guess. That's how it was on the third day of my visit to the future year of 802,701 A.D.—lots of mysteries and no answers to my questions. But it was a pretty good day anyhow, because I made a friend.

"It happened that earlier that morning I was watching some of the little people bathing in the river. One of them got a cramp and started sinking under the water. When I saw this little person drowning, I quickly slipped off my coat and dove in to save her. I caught the poor tiny thing and drew her safely to land. After I rubbed her arms and legs, she was all right. I felt good that I had been able to save her life.

"Later that afternoon I met this same little woman as I was taking one of my walks. She greeted me with happy cries and gave me some flowers she had picked for me. I was quite pleased, for I had been feeling lonely. I thanked her for the gift, and soon we were sitting together having a talk, which was mostly smiles.

"We passed each other flowers, and she kissed my hands. I did the same to hers. Then I tried talking in some of the words I had learned. I found out that her name was Weena. I don't know what it meant, although it somehow seemed to fit her just right.

"That was the beginning of a strange friendship. You shall see later that it ended more sadly than it began.

"She was exactly like a child. She wanted to be with me all the time. She tried to follow me everywhere. If ever I left her behind during my walks, she called sadly after me. She was sometimes more a bother than anything. But she was also a great comfort at times. I did not know what I meant to her, nor did I understand how much I cared about her—until it was too late.

"It was from her that I learned that fear still existed in this future world. She was brave enough in the daylight, but she was terribly afraid of the dark, afraid of shadows, and afraid of black things. Darkness was the one thing that scared her. It was such a strong fear that it made me curious. I began watching more closely.

"I discovered that these little people gathered into the large houses after dark and slept in large groups. They became upset if I walked in on them without a light. I never found one of them alone after dark.

"From then on, little Weena slept with her head resting on my arm. You will hear more about Weena later, but now I must get back to my story.

CHAPTER NINE

The Morlocks

"I think it was the night before I saved Weena that I had a terrible nightmare. I dreamed that I was drowning and ugly sea creatures were pawing over my face with their soft feelers. I woke up with a jolt! Then I had a strange feeling that some grayish animal had just rushed out of the room. I tried to get to sleep again, but I felt too frightened. I got up and went outside.

"The moon was setting and the dying moonlight gave a ghostly color to everything. The bushes were inky black and the ground was a dark gray. Up on the hill I thought I could see ghosts. Several times I saw weird, white figures. Twice I thought I saw

an ape-like animal running rather quickly up the hill. Near the old buildings, I saw three of them carrying some dark body. They moved quickly and I did not see where they went. Had they hid among the bushes? Since it was not quite daylight, I didn't know if I could believe my eyes or not.

"As the sky grew brighter and daylight came, I studied the hillside again. I saw no sign of the white figures. I was thinking of this all that morning, until Weena's rescue from the river drove them out of my head. Do you remember earlier when I thought I had seen a deer? Well, now I began to think maybe it had been something else—something much stranger. The white figures that looked like apes never left my mind after that.

"One very hot morning, another frightening thing happened. I was looking for some shelter from the heat in a huge ruined building near the big house where I slept and ate. Scrambling among these piles of stone and concrete, I found a narrow covered hall. Fallen stones blocked the windows and the hall was terribly dark. I went in, feeling my way along. Suddenly I stopped, frozen with terror. A pair of gleaming eyes was watching me out of the darkness.

"I was sure these were the eyes of some wild beast. I clenched my hands and stared into the glaring eyeballs. I was afraid to turn. Finally, getting over my fear a little, I took a step forward and spoke. Then I put out my hand and touched something soft.

"At once the eyes darted sideways and something white ran past me. With my heart in my mouth, I turned and saw an odd ape-like figure. It held its head down in a strange way as it ran around behind me. It stumbled into a block of stone and staggered aside. In the next second it was hidden in a black shadow under a pile of concrete.

"My memory of it is not perfect, but I know it was a dull white, and had strange, large, grayish-red eyes. There was golden hair on its head and down its back. But it went too fast for me to see clearly. After a second or two, I followed it into the pile of ruins.

"I could not find it at first, but after a while I came to one of those round well openings I have told you about. A sudden thought came to me. Could this strange Thing have gone down the hole of the well?

"I lit a match and peered into the well. There I saw a small, white creature with large bright eyes that watched me as it backed away. It made me shiver. Like a human spider, it was scampering down the wall of the well on a metal ladder. Then the match burned my fingers and fell out of my hand. By the time I had lit another, the little monster was gone.

"I do not know how long I sat staring down that well. It was some time before I could make myself believe that the Thing I had seen was human. But slowly the truth came to me. Man must have changed into *two* different animals in this future time. The pretty little people of the Upper-world were not the only things living here. That white, ape-like night beast lived here, too—somewhere beneath the earth, in an Under-world.

"Now I thought I knew the truth about those horrible gray wells. What else was hiding in that hole? I knew I would have to go down into the well to figure things out. I sat on the edge, telling myself that there was nothing to fear. But—I *was* afraid to go! I began thinking again about those doors in the base of the White Sphinx. I was sure now where my Time Machine was and who had taken it.

"As I thought more about it, I was certain that the ape-like creatures lived under the earth. There were three things which made me think that. They had the pale, white look of animals that live mostly in the dark—like the white fish of the Kentucky caves, for instance. They had those large eyes often seen in night animals such as owls. Lastly, the white creatures always ran toward the darkness and held their heads down in the light. The light must hurt their eyes because they weren't used to it.

"So, if these things lived under the ground, the earth must be full of tunnels. And these tunnels must be home to these white creatures. The many wells told me that tunnels must be everywhere in

the Under-world. But what were these Under-world creatures? And what do they do?

"As I said, I thought that over hundreds of thousands of years, the way man looked must have slowly changed. Over all those years the little people of the Upper-world and the creatures of the Under-world must have become two quite different types of Man—two different animals. In the end, there were the little lazy people who lived in pleasure, comfort, and beauty. These were the Upper-worlders. They called themselves the 'Eloi.' And there were the white, ape-like creatures who had learned to live in the dark. These were the Under-worlders—who were called 'Morlocks.'

"So, this was my *new* idea about the future world and its people. As you shall see, I had more to learn. I still knew very little about the Under-world and its Morlocks. I still had questions that worried me.

"Why had the Morlocks taken my Time Machine? And why were the Eloi so terribly afraid of the dark?

"I asked Weena about this Under-world, but she would not answer me. She shivered as though she could not stand to talk about it and burst into tears. They were the only tears, except my own, I ever saw in that Golden Age of the Future. When I saw them, I stopped bothering her about the Morlocks and only wanted her to stop crying. Soon she was smiling and clapping her hands, while I burned matches to make her laugh.

CHAPTER TEN

Down into the Well

"It may seem odd to you, but it was two days before I could bring myself to think about the wells. I wanted to stay away from those white Things. They were the same pale color of worms and animals I had seen in bottles in a science museum. And they were sickeningly cold to the touch. I soon found out that the Eloi also hated the Morlocks.

"The next night I did not sleep well. My stomach was a little upset and I was full of worry. Once or twice I had a feeling of intense fear for no clear reason. Maybe it was because the moon would become just a sliver, in a few days, and the nights would grow darker. This was when those ugly white monkeys from below might appear more often. I don't know if you will understand my feeling, but I never felt quite safe when I thought what might be waiting just behind me. I kept on looking around this new place, anyway.

"I came upon a huge green building that looked like a palace. It was larger than any of the buildings I had seen, and the outside had an Oriental look. The face of it had the shine and bluish-green color of fine dishes from China, called porcelain. I wondered what this strange building could have been used for. I thought it must have a special use, and I wanted to go in and look around. But I had found the place after a long and tiring trip and it was getting late. I decided to wait to explore this Palace of Green Porcelain the next day. I then returned for the night to the Eloi building and the friendship of little Weena.

"As I walked back, I began to think that I was just putting off the thing I did not want to do. So I made up my mind that the next day I would not visit the Palace. Instead, I had to go down into that mysterious Under-world—down into a well!

"Early the next morning I started out toward a well near the ruins of granite and aluminum. Little Weena ran with me. She danced beside me to the well, but when she saw me lean over the edge and look down she seemed scared and confused.

" 'Good-bye, Little Weena,' I said, kissing her. Then I began to feel over the sides of the wall for the ladder. Weena gave a most sad cry. Running to me, she began to pull at me with her little hands. I shook her off, and in another moment I was in the well. I saw her sad face over the wall's edge and I smiled to comfort her. Then I looked down at the wobbly hooks of the ladder on which I would have to hang.

"I had to crawl down a hole of perhaps six hundred feet. I could not forget, of course, that this ladder was made for creatures much lighter and smaller than me. One of the hooks bent suddenly and almost swung me off into the blackness below.

"For a few seconds I hung by one hand. My arms and back were full of pain, but I went on down the deep hole. I looked up at the opening at the top of the well. Little Weena's head looked like a round black dot peeking over the edge.

"The grinding, bumping sound of a machine below grew louder. Everything except that little hole at the top of the well was completely dark. When I looked up again, Weena was gone.

"At last, I saw below me, about a foot to the right, a small opening in the side of the wall. Swinging myself in, I found I was in a narrow tunnel. It was level enough for me to lie down and finally rest. It had come just in time. My arms ached, my back was cramped, and I was trembling with the terror of falling.

"I do not know how long I lay there. I was wakened by something touching my face. I grabbed for my matches and quickly lit one. I saw three slouching white creatures like the one I had seen above ground. They were backing away from the light of my match. I was sure they could see me in the darkness, and they did not seem to have any fear of me. But, as soon as I struck a match they ran away out of control into the dark tunnels. Their eyes glared out at me from their hiding places.

"I tried to call to them, but their language must have been different from that of the Upper-world people. I wondered what to do, and the thought of scrambling back up the well passed through my mind. But I said to myself, 'You are in it to stay, now.' Feeling my way along the tunnel, I heard the noise of machinery grow louder. I struck another match and saw that I had entered a large cave which stretched into total darkness.

"You will understand that my memory is not completely clear. I *do* know that in the gloom I saw the shapes of big machines that made horrible black shadows. I saw ghostly Morlocks hide from the light of my match in these shadows. The place was very stuffy and damp. The faint smell of fresh blood was in the air. Some distance away I saw a table on which sat a big piece of meat. The Morlocks must be meat-eaters! What animal had this red roast of meat come from? It was all very unclear and scary—the heavy smell, the big gray shapes, the ugly Morlocks hiding in the shadows, just waiting for the darkness when they could try to attack me. Then the match burned my fingers and fell from my hand. It looked like a wriggling red spot in the blackness.

"If only I had thought to bring a camera! I could have flashed a picture of the Under-world in a second and studied it carefully later on. But, as it was, I stood there with only the things that Nature had given me—hands, feet, and teeth. That is all I had—plus the four safety matches I still had left. Suddenly, I felt a hand on my head.

"Long, thin fingers came feeling over my face, and there was a strange, unpleasant smell. I thought I heard the breathing of a crowd of those horrible little creatures around me. I felt the box of matches being tugged at in my hand while something behind me was picking at my clothing.

"I shouted as loudly as I could, but the beasts just kept coming toward me. They clutched at me, whispering strange sounds to each other. I shivered terribly and shouted again. This time they made a strange, gurgling, laughing noise as they came back at me.

"I lit another match and the creatures backed away. I was able to slip into a narrow tunnel, but just as I did my match blew out! In the blackness I could hear the Morlocks' pitter-pattering footsteps coming after me again.

"In an instant, I was grabbed by several hands trying to pull me from the tunnel. I struck another light and waved it in their faces. The flare of my match blinded and confused them. You cannot believe how horrible and ghastly they looked. They had pale, chinless faces and huge, lidless, pinkish-gray eyes. They made me feel sick in my stomach, and I did not stay to study them, I promise you! I backed up again, and when my second match went out, I struck my third. It had almost burned out by the time I got out of the side tunnel and back to the well hole.

"I lay still for a moment. The throb of the great, grinding machines below made me dizzy and weak. Then I felt sideways for the ladder. Just as I did, my feet were grabbed from behind and I was yanked backward! I struck my last match, which would not stay lit. But I had my hand on the climbing hooks now. Kicking as hard as I could, I got myself loose from the clutches of the Morlocks. I began hurrying up the ladder. The white creatures stayed below, staring and blinking up at me. One little beast, however, followed me for a short way and almost stole my shoe as a prize.

"I thought I would never get to the top of the well! An awful, sick feeling came over me and I almost lost my hold on the ladder. The last few yards I had to fight to keep from fainting. Somehow I got over the top edge of the well and staggered out into the blinding sunlight.

"I fell on my face. The soil smelled sweet and clean. I remember Weena kissing my hands and ears. Then I became more dizzy—and I fainted.

CHAPTER ELEVEN

Wanderings

"When I awoke from my faint, I felt like an animal caught in a trap. And now I had to face another kind of enemy—the darkness of the nights as the moon became smaller.

"Weena had talked mysteriously about the Dark Nights. I knew that over the next few nights the moon would be but a sliver in the sky—and we would have Dark Nights. And now I understood why the little Eloi of the Upper-world were so afraid of the dark. For it was in the dark that the Morlocks came out.

"I wondered what horrible things the Morlocks did under the very darkest night skies.

"I thought more about the Eloi's fears and their hatred of the Morlocks. Then, for some reason, I remembered the meat I had seen on the table in the Under-world. It seemed odd how it popped into my mind. I tried to think what the meat had looked like. It looked like something I had seen before, but I could not think what it was at the time.

"I felt I could never sleep again until my bed was safe from the Morlocks. I knew I had to get some weapons and a safe place to sleep. I shuddered with horror to think how they must already have watched me in the dark.

"I wandered during the afternoon along the valley of a river, but found no place that I thought was safe. I knew the Morlocks were skillful climbers, for I had seen how they scrambled around the well. All the buildings and trees seemed within their easy reach. Then I happened to recall the Palace of Green Porcelain. Perhaps this was a spot to look into.

"In the evening I took Weena like a child on my shoulder. We went up the hills toward the southwest in the direction of the Palace. I had figured this would be a seven or eight mile walk, but it must have been nearer eighteen.

"To make the long walk worse, the heel of one of my shoes was loose and a nail was coming through and into my foot. I was limping badly. So, it was already early evening when I finally saw the Palace in the distance.

"Weena had been happy when I began to carry her. But after a while she asked me to let her down. She ran along by my side, now and then darting off to pick flowers to stick in my pockets. My pockets had always puzzled Weena. Finally, she had decided that they were some strange kind of flower vase—at least she used them for that. And that reminds me! In changing my jacket this evening I found…"

The Time Traveler stopped talking for a moment, put his hand into his pocket, and silently placed two large, white, withered flowers on the little table. Then he went back to his story.

"The hush of evening crept over the world as we traveled over the hill. Weena grew tired and wanted to return to the house of gray stone. But I pointed to the Palace of Green Porcelain in the distance and tried to make her understand that we were looking for a place where she would be safe from her Fear.

"You know how quiet it gets at twilight? Even the breeze stops in the trees. It was just that way then. The sky was clear and empty except for a few purple lines in the sunset. I felt as though I could feel the hollowness of the ground under my feet. I could imagine the Morlocks below me, scurrying around like ants, waiting for the dark.

"So we went on, and the twilight turned into night. One star after another came out. The ground grew gray and the trees black. Weena's fears and tiredness grew. I took her in my arms and hugged her. Then, as it got even darker, she put her arms around my neck. She closed her eyes and pressed her face against my shoulder. So far, I had seen nothing of the Morlocks, but it was still early in the night. The darkest hours were still to come.

"From the top of the next hill I saw a thick forest spreading wide and black in front of me. I stopped. Feeling tired—my feet, especially, were very sore— I carefully lowered Weena from my shoulder and sat down on the grass. I could no longer see the Palace of Green Porcelain, and I was unsure of where it was. I looked into the thick woods and wondered what it might hide. Even if there were no white beasts—which I did not want to even think about—

there would be roots and trees to stumble over. I decided that I would not go into the woods. We would spend the night there on the open hill.

"Weena, I was glad to see, was sound asleep. I carefully wrapped her in my jacket and sat down beside her to wait for the moonrise. The hillside was quiet and lonely, but from the black forest came the sounds of living things moving around. Above me the stars shone, for the night was very clear. I felt a friendly comfort in their twinkling.

"Looking at these stars, my own troubles and all the problems of life on Earth seemed small. I looked at little Weena sleeping beside me. I looked at her again, and suddenly I thought I knew what the meat might be that I had seen down in the well. Yet it was too horrible to think of! It couldn't be, could it? I shivered and tried to put the idea out of my mind.

"Through that long night I tried to keep my mind off the Morlocks and passed the time counting stars. The sky stayed very clear, except for a hazy cloud or two. I took some catnaps. Soon a faint light came in the eastern sky and the old moon rose, thin, pointed, and white. And close behind came the dawn, pale at first, then growing pink and warm.

"No Morlocks had bothered us and I had seen none on the hill that night. In the friendly light of the new day it almost seemed to me that I had made too much of my fear. I stood up and saw that my foot with the bad shoe had become swollen at the ankle and painful under the heel. So I sat down again, took off my shoes, and threw them away.

"I awakened Weena and we went down into the woods, now green and pleasant instead of black and frightening. We found some fruit and had our breakfast. We soon met others of the little Eloi laughing and dancing in the sunlight, as though there were no such thing in nature as the night.

"Then I thought once more of the meat that I had seen. I was sure now what it was. I believe that some time in the Long Ago, the Morlocks had run out of food in their Under-world. They might have lived on rats and other such things for a while. But not now! The Eloi had become their food. The Eloi were like well-fed beef cattle which the Morlocks killed and brought to their dinner table.

"From the bottom of my heart I felt sorry for these pretty little people. And there was little Weena dancing at my side!

"I had no idea what to do next. I knew I still needed to find a safe place. I needed to make myself some weapons of metal, or stone, or whatever I could find. I hoped to find some way of making fire so that I would have the weapons of flames and light. For, as I have told you, nothing I knew of worked better against those Morlocks. Then I wanted to find a way to break open the doors of bronze under the White Sphinx. I was sure that if I could enter those doors carrying a blaze of light, I would find the Time Machine and escape.

"I decided that, when I *did* find the Time Machine, I would bring Weena back here with me—back through Time, back to this very house. Turning these ideas over in my mind, I led the way toward the Palace of Green Porcelain.

CHAPTER TWELVE

The Palace of Green Porcelain

"Around noon we came to the Palace sitting high on a hill. It was empty and falling down into ruins. Only ragged bits of glass were left in its windows. Some of the green covering had fallen away from the rusted metal frame.

"As we came closer, I saw that the outside surface really *was* made of porcelain. I saw some writing on it in some unknown letters. I thought that Weena might help me to read this, but I learned that the idea of writing had never entered her head. She always seemed to me, I guess, more human than she really was, perhaps because her love was so human.

"We went through the big doors, which were broken and open. Inside we found a long hall of displays and exhibits. It must have been an old museum. The floor was thick with dust, and a huge collection of objects was covered in the same gray dust. Standing in the center of the long room was a strange sight. It was the bony skeleton of some creature I had never before seen. Further on was the skeleton of a huge Brontosaurus.

"Everywhere along the sides were shelves and glass cases full of ancient fossils of every kind. Some were well preserved and in good condition. Weena, who had been rolling an old seashell down the sloping glass of a case, now took my hand and stood quietly beside me.

"Exploring a bit further, I found another short hall. This area appeared to be a collection of minerals. I thought I might be lucky and find some things to make gunpowder. But, finding none, I headed down yet another hall. It looked as though this had been the natural history section, but there was not much left of it. There were a few shriveled remains of animals that had been stuffed. There were some dried mummies and the brown dust of dead plants—that was all.

"Next we came to a room of great size, but very dark. I was more at home here, for on either side of me were the huge frames of big machines. All were badly rusted and many were broken down, but some were still fairly complete. As you all know, I have a strong interest in machines, but I could not figure out what any of these had been used for.

"Suddenly, Weena came very close to my side—so suddenly that she startled me. Had it not been for her I don't think I would have noticed that it had become darker. I had been too interested in the machines. Poor Weena became frightened as she saw the thick darkness ahead of us. I stopped and looked around.

"I saw that the dust on the floor had been broken by a number of small, narrow footprints. My mind went to the Morlocks, and I thought they might be somewhere near. I felt that I was wasting my time studying the machinery. It was already late in the afternoon and I had still no weapon, no safe place to sleep, and no way of making a fire. Then, down in the deep blackness of the hall, I heard a strange patter, patter, patter of small feet—the same weird noises I had heard down in the well!

"I took Weena's hand. Then, struck with an idea, I left her and went to a machine that had a metal handle. Climbing up and grabbing this handle in my hands, I put all my weight on it. Soon it snapped and broke off. At last, I had a weapon—an iron bar plenty big enough to club any Morlock I came across. And I wanted very much to fight a Morlock or two! So, iron bar in one hand and Weena in the other, I went out of that room.

"We entered a still larger room filled with what was left of old, ragged books. Then, going up a broad staircase, we came to what once was a chemistry display. Here I thought I might find something I could use. I searched through every unbroken case. At last, in one of the airtight cases, I found a box of matches. Becoming very excited, I tried them. They worked just fine! Now I had another good weapon against the horrible Morlocks.

"I turned to Weena. 'A dance!' I cried to her in her own language. And so, in that ancient, run-down museum, on the thick, soft carpet of dust, and to Weena's huge delight, I performed a kind of dance, whistling as cheerfully as I could. It was part can-can, part swing, and part my own invention. For I *love* to invent things, as you gentlemen know.

"As we went around the corner into the next room I found something even more surprising than the matches. In a sealed, dry jar was something that looked like wax. When I broke the jar I could tell by its smell that it was camphor. I was about to throw it aside, but I remembered that camphor burned with a good bright flame, like a candle, so I put it in my pocket.

"I found no explosives or any other tool for breaking down the bronze doors. So far, my iron bar was the best thing I had come across. Still, I left that room very excited.

"I went through room after room. As the evening went on, I began to lose interest. Most of the displays were nothing more than heaps of rust. After a while, we came to a little open courtyard within the Palace. It was grassy and had three fruit trees. Here we rested and ate some of the sweet fruit. Toward sunset, I began to think about what to do next.

"Night was coming and I had still not found a safe hiding place. But that troubled me very little now. I had something that was the best protection from the Morlocks—I had matches! And I had the camphor in my pocket if I needed a brighter flame. In the morning I would go after my Time Machine. To do that, I had only my iron bar. But the doors hadn't looked very strong, and I thought I could pry them open. Only then would I learn the secrets of the White Sphinx. And maybe I would understand its mysterious smile.

CHAPTER THIRTEEN

Into the Dark Woods

"We left the Palace while the sun was just starting to set. I wanted to reach the White Sphinx early the next morning, so I pushed on toward the woods. My plan was to go as far as possible that night, build a fire, and sleep in the protection of its glaring flames. As we went along I gathered any sticks or dried grass I saw and soon had my arms full. It was the middle of the night before we reached the woods. Weena, afraid of the darkness before us, wanted to stop outside the woods' edge. I had a feeling of danger and felt we must keep going. I soon became so tired that I knew sleep was creeping up on me—*and so were the Morlocks!*

"Just as we entered the woods, I saw three crouching shadows in the black bushes behind us. With bushes and long grass all around us, I did not feel safe. The forest, I figured, was a little less than a mile across. If we could get through it to the bare hillside, it seemed to me we would find a safer resting place. With my matches and my camphor I could light our path through the woods. But, if I was waving matches with my hands, I couldn't carry the sticks for a fire, so I put them down. When I did I got an idea. I would surprise the evil Morlocks by lighting a fire! I found out later what a foolish idea this turned out to be. But at the time it seemed a clever way to keep from being followed.

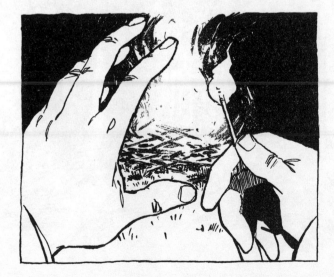

"The red tongues of fire went licking up my pile of wood. This was a new and strange thing to Weena. She wanted to run to it and play with it. I believe she would have thrown herself into it if I had not held her back. But I caught her up and rushed ahead into the woods. For a little way the glare of my fire lit the path. Looking back, I could see that the flames from my pile of sticks had spread to some nearby bushes and a line of fire was creeping up the grass of the hill. I laughed at that, and turned again to the trees ahead.

"It was very dark and Weena clung to me, frightened. Overhead, the sky was completely black. I couldn't light my matches because I had no free hand. On my left arm I carried my little Weena, in my right hand I held my iron bar.

"For some time I heard nothing but the cracking twigs under my feet, the faint rustle of the wind, my own breathing, and the throbbing of my blood in my ears. Then I seemed to hear that terrible pattering sound again. I stumbled on. The pattering grew clearer and I heard the same voices I had heard in the tunnels of the Under-world. There must have been several of the Morlocks—and they were closing in on me.

"In another minute I felt something pull at my coat, then at my arm. Weena shivered terribly and became quite still.

"It was time for a match. But to get one I had to put poor Weena down. With my hand free, I fumbled with my pocket. Then in the darkness, around my knees a struggle began between a silent Weena and the strangely cooing Morlocks. Hands began creeping over my coat and back, even touching my neck. Then the match scratched, fizzed, and flared. I saw the white backs of the Morlocks running away among the trees.

"I quickly took a lump of camphor from my pocket and was ready to light it as soon as the match began to go out. Then I looked at Weena.

"She was lying completely still at my feet, her face to the ground. With a sudden fright I bent down to her. I could not tell if she was breathing or not. I lit the block of camphor and threw it to the ground. It split and flamed up, driving back the Morlocks and the shadows. The woods behind seemed full of the stir and murmur of a great many things as I lifted up little Weena. She seemed to have fainted.

"I put her carefully on my shoulder and rose to go on. But in what direction? I had turned myself around several times, and now I had no idea where my path was. For all I knew, I might be facing back toward the Palace of Green Porcelain. I had to think quickly what to do. I decided to build a fire and camp where we were.

"I put Weena down again. As fast as I could, I began collecting sticks and leaves. Here and there, out of the darkness around me, the Morlocks' eyes shone like red jewels.

"The camphor flickered and went out. I lit a match. As I did, two white forms that had been coming toward Weena dashed away. One was so blinded by the light that he came straight for me, and I felt his bones crunch under the blow of my fist. He gave a whoop of shock, staggered a little way, and fell down. I lit another piece of camphor and went on gathering things for my bonfire. Very soon I had a smoky fire of green wood and dry sticks, and could save my camphor for later.

"Then I turned to where Weena lay beside my iron bar. I tried to waken her, but she looked as if she were dead.

"The smoke of the fire blew over toward me, and it must have made me suddenly tired. My fire would not need more wood for an hour or so. I felt very weary after my struggles and sat down. The forest was also full of a sleepy murmur that I did not understand.

"I seemed only to nod off to sleep for a second, but when I opened my eyes all was dark, and the Morlocks had their hands on me. Flinging off their clinging fingers, I felt in my pocket for the matchbox, and—*it was gone!*

CHAPTER FOURTEEN

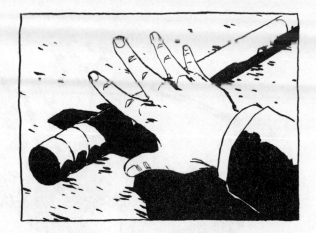

Fear and Fire

"The Morlocks grabbed me again. And in a moment I knew what had happened. I had slept, and my fire had gone out—although the forest behind me still smelled of burning wood. I was caught by the neck, by the hair, by the arms, and was pulled down. It was horrible in the darkness to feel all these creatures creeping over me. I felt as if I were in a giant spider's web. Little teeth began nipping at my neck. I rolled over and my hand brushed against my iron bar! I struggled up, shook the human rats from me, and swung my bar. I could feel the juicy squish of flesh and bone under my blows, and for now I was free.

"Then I lost control. My anger and fear took hold of me. I would not give up. I would fight. I decided to make the Morlocks pay for their murders and their Eloi meat.

"I stood with my back to a tree, swinging the iron bar at the monsters in front of me. The whole forest was full of them. A minute passed, and their voices seemed to grow more excited as their movements grew faster. Yet none came within reach. I stood glaring at the blackness.

"Then I had a thought that gave me hope. Maybe the Morlocks were afraid! The darkness seemed to grow brighter. Very dimly I began to see the Morlocks around me—three battered and bruised at my feet—and then I was shocked to see that the others were running away. Their backs seemed no longer white, but reddish-orange. As I stood amazed, I saw a little red spark go drifting between the tree branches. And then I understood the smell of burning wood, the loud roar, and the red glow. And I knew why the Morlocks were running away.

"Stepping out from behind my tree and looking back, I saw that the first bonfire I had made had set the whole forest on fire.

"I looked for Weena, but she was gone. The hissing and crackling behind me and the whoosh and pop as each fresh tree burst into flame left little time to think. Still tightly holding my iron bar, I followed in the Morlocks' path. It was a close race. But at last I came to a small open space. One Morlock went stumbling past me, straight into the fire!

"And now I was to see, I think, the most weird and horrible thing of all that I saw in that future age. Upon the hillside were thirty or forty Morlocks, dazzled by the light and heat. They were staggering here and there against each other in their fear and blindness. At first I did not understand and struck wildly at them with my bar, killing one and injuring several more. But then I saw the helplessness of one of them rolling around under the burning tree and heard their cries. I realized their total blindness and pain caused by the glaring light. I struck no more of them.

"Still, every now and then one of these miserable Morlocks would come straight toward me, giving me a quivering horror that made me quick to get out of the way. Once, the flames died down and I was afraid the awful creatures would soon be able to see me. I was thinking of beginning the fight once more, but the fire burst out again brightly and I held back. I walked around the hill, staying away from them, looking for some small sign of Weena. But Weena was gone!

"I found myself hoping it was a nightmare. I bit myself and screamed, trying to wake up. I beat the ground with my hands, got up and sat down again. I stumbled here and there, and again sat down. Then I tried rubbing my eyes and calling upon God to let me wake from this bad dream. Three times I saw Morlocks put their heads down in a kind of agony and rush into the flames.

"At last, above the dying red of the fire, above the clouds of black smoke and dying tree stumps, came the white light of the day. Only a few of the beasts were left.

"I searched again for clues of Weena, but there were none. They must have left her poor little body in the forest. I cannot describe how thankful I was to think that she had not ended up on the Morlocks' dinner table. As I thought of that, I wanted to kill every one of the helpless, hateful creatures around me, but once again, I held myself back. I could see the Palace of Green Porcelain through the smoke. From that I could figure out in which direction to head for the White Sphinx.

"As the day grew clearer, I tied some grass around my feet and limped on across smoking ashes toward the Sphinx, the hiding place of the Time Machine. I walked slowly, for I was nearly worn out, and I felt a sad pain over losing little Weena. Now, sitting here with you in this old familiar room, it is more like the sadness of a dream than a real loss. But that morning it left me terribly alone. I began to think of this house of mine, of this fireside, of some of you. I was suddenly very homesick.

"But as I walked on under the bright morning sky, I made a discovery. In my pocket were some loose matches. They must have fallen out of the box before it was lost. They gave me the strength and hope to continue.

CHAPTER FIFTEEN

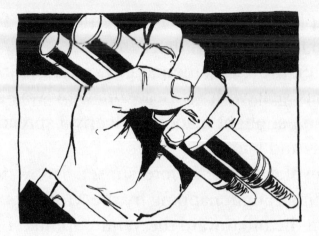

The Sphinx Smiles

"About eight or nine in the morning, I came to the same seat of yellow metal from which I had seen this world on the evening I arrived.

"Here was the same beautiful scene—the same trees and plants, the same fine large buildings. The colorful robes of the Eloi moved here and there among the trees. Some were bathing in the river where I had saved Weena, and I felt a sharp pain of sadness. And there were those hideous, grinding wells of the Under-world. I understood now the terror of the wells and what lived in them below the ground. And I also knew the awful truth about the little Upper-world people. Very pleasant was their day, as pleasant as the day of cattle being fattened up. And their end was the same.

"After the excitements and terrors of the past days, this seat with its peaceful view was a relief. The warm sunlight made me sleepy. I spread out on the grass and had a long sleep.

"I awoke a little before sunset. I now felt safe from being caught napping by the Morlocks. I came on down the hill toward the White Sphinx. I had my iron bar in one hand, and the other hand played with the matches in my pocket.

"And now came a most surprising thing. As I got nearer the base of the smiling Sphinx, I found the bronze doors were open! At that I stopped short in front of them. Waiting a moment, I entered.

"Inside was a small room, and in the corner was the Time Machine! So here, after all my plans for an attack on the White Sphinx, was a quiet surrender. I threw my iron bar away, almost sorry not to use it.

"A sudden thought came into my head. This was probably just a trap set by the Morlocks. Holding back a strong desire to laugh, I walked over to the Time Machine. I was surprised to find it had been carefully oiled and cleaned.

"Then came the thing I thought would happen. The bronze doors suddenly slid shut, striking the frame with a clang. I was in the dark, trapped—or so the Morlocks thought! I smiled as I thought of the levers in my pocket which would get the Time Machine and me out of there.

"I could already hear their murmuring laughter as the white creatures came toward me. They thought they had tricked me. Very calmly, I pulled out a match. All I had to do was put the levers on the machine and leave like a ghost. But I had missed one little thing. The matches were that terrible kind that light only on the box, *and I no longer had the box!*

"You can imagine my fright. The little beasts were closing in on me. I swung at them in the dark and began to scramble into the saddle of the machine. Then a hand touched me, and then another. I had to fight against their grabbing fingers as I tried to get the levers hooked up to the machine. They almost got one lever away from me. As it slipped from my hand, I had to ram in the dark with my head (I could hear the Morlock's skull ring) to get it back.

"I was finally able to get both levers fastened and gave one a hard pull. The clinging, ape-like hands slipped away from me. The darkness fell from my eyes. Suddenly I was time traveling again. I found myself in the same gray whirl that I described to you before.

CHAPTER SIXTEEN

Into the Far Future

"I have already told you of the sickness and dizziness that comes with time traveling. And this time I was not seated firmly in the saddle. For a time I clung to the machine as it swayed and shook, quite unsure of what I was doing. When I looked at the dials again I was shocked to see what I had done. One dial shows days traveled, another thousands of days, another millions. Instead of putting the levers in reverse to go *backward* in Time, I had pulled them into the *forward* position. Now the thousand-day dial was whirling around so fast it was just a blur. Instead of going back home, I was flying like a tornado further into the future!

"Things grew black as I flew faster and faster through Time. The changes from day to night got slower and slower. I realized that the sun no longer set. I finally got my hands on the levers again and began to slow the machine down. Slower and slower went the circling hands on the dials until they came to a stop. I could see I was on a lonely beach somewhere in the far distant future. I sat on the machine and looked around.

"The rocks around me were a reddish color, and the only sign of life that I could see at first were the green plants that covered them. It was the same rich green that you see on forest moss or on the fungus in caves. There were no waves on the sea. It just rose and fell with a soft swell, like a gentle breathing. Along the edge was a thick crust of salt.

"Far away up the beach I heard a sharp screech and saw a thing like a huge white butterfly go fluttering up into the sky and disappear over some low hills. The sound of its voice was so weird that I shivered and held more tightly to the machine. Looking around me again, I saw a pile of red rocks start to move slowly toward me. Then I saw that it was really a monstrous crab-like creature. Can you picture a crab as large as a table, many legs moving slowly, big claws swaying, long feelers waving, and its eyes on stalks gleaming at you on either side of its body? I could see the long feelers that stuck out from its mouth, flicking and touching as it moved.

"As I stared at this ugly crawling thing, I felt a tickling on my cheek as if a fly had landed there. I tried to brush it away with my hand. In a moment it came back, and there was another tickling my ear. I swatted and caught something slimy—*that slid out of my hand*. Scared to death, I turned and saw I had grabbed the feeler of another monster crab that stood just behind me. Its evil eyes were wriggling on their stalks, its hungry mouth was open, and its huge, slime-covered claws were snapping and reaching toward me. In a second my hand was on the lever, and I got out of there.

"I moved on another hundred years. But there was the same beach, the same crabs creeping in and out among the green weeds.

"So I traveled on in great leaps of a thousand years or more, drawn on by the mystery of the earth's future. At last, more than thirty million years later, I stopped once more. The crawling crabs were gone and the red beach, except for its green fungus, seemed lifeless. I looked around.

"The green slime on the rocks was the only sign of anything living. White flakes of strange snow were falling all around. I thought I saw some black object flopping around on a sandbank, but it stopped moving as I looked at it. I was sure my eyes were playing tricks and that the black object was only a rock. The stars in the sky were extremely bright, but seemed to twinkle very little.

"The horror of this lonely future world finally hit me. I shivered and felt sick to my stomach. I got off the machine to steady myself. I felt dizzy and unable to face the return trip. As I stood, sick and scared, I saw again the thing on the sandbank. There was no mistake now. It *was* a moving thing. It was round, the size of a football or maybe bigger, and long, snake-like feelers hung down from it.

"The thing looked black against the rolling, blood-red water, and it was eerily flopping about on the sand. I felt myself fainting. But a terrible fear of lying helpless in that lonely world gave me the strength to somehow climb back into the seat of the Time Machine.

CHAPTER SEVENTEEN

Back Home—In Time for Dinner

"So I came back home. For a long time I must have been numb upon the machine. The blinking on and off between days and nights began once more. The sun became golden again, the sky blue. I breathed with greater freedom. The hands spun backward on the dials. At last I saw again the dim shadows of houses. These changed and passed, and others came. When the millions dial was at zero, I reduced my speed. I began to see our own simple houses. Then the thousands hand ran back to zero, and the night and day flapped slower and slower. The old walls of the laboratory came round me. Very gently, now, I slowed the machine down.

"I saw one little thing that seemed odd to me. I think I have told you that when I first started the Time Machine from here, Mrs. Watchett had walked across the room. She had moved, it seemed to me, like a rocket. As I returned, I passed again across that point in Time when she crossed the workshop. But now her every move was the exact opposite of before. She was walking quietly across the workshop—*backward*—out the door she had come in.

"Then I stopped the machine, and saw about me again the old familiar workshop and my tools, just as I had left them. I got off the thing shaky, and sat down on my bench. For several minutes I trembled. Then I became calmer. Around me was my old workshop again, exactly as it had been. Maybe I had slept there and the whole thing had been a dream… But then I noticed something that told me I had not been dreaming.

"The machine had started from the left wall of the workshop. It had come to a stop again against the *right* wall—where you can go see it now. That gives you the exact distance the Morlocks had moved my machine—from the little lawn to the base of the White Sphinx.

"For a time my brain went numb. After a while I got up and came through the hall here, limping, because my heel was still painful, and feeling terribly dirty.

"I saw a newspaper on the table by the door. I found the date was indeed today. Looking at the clock, I saw the time was almost eight o'clock. I heard your voices and the rattling of dinner plates. I waited—I felt so sick and weak. Then I smelled good meat and opened the door to find you all sitting here. You know the rest. I washed, and ate, and now I am telling you the story.

"I know," he said, "that all this will be unbelievable to you. To *me* the one unbelievable thing is that I am here tonight in this old familiar room, looking into your friendly faces and telling you of these strange adventures."

He glanced at the doubting face of the Doctor and said, "No. I cannot expect you to believe it. Take it as a lie—or as a prediction of the future. You can say I dreamed it in the workshop. You can take it all as just a story I've made up to tell my theories about man in the future… And taking it as a story, what do you think of it?"

The Time Traveler walked over to the fireplace and, in his usual manner, began to stir the fire.

Everyone was silent for a few minutes. Shoes scraped nervously on the carpet. I took my eyes off the Time Traveler's face and looked around at the other guests. The Doctor seemed to be studying the Time Traveler. The Editor was looking hard at the end of his cigar. The Journalist fumbled for his watch. The others, as far as I remember, didn't move a muscle.

The Editor stood up with a sigh. "What a shame it is you're not a writer of stories!" he said, putting his hand on the Time Traveler's shoulder.

"You don't believe it?"

"Well—"

"I thought not. To tell you the truth… I hardly believe it myself… And yet…"

His eyes moved to the withered white flowers on the little table. As he pointed to them I saw him look down at the half-healed scars on his knuckles.

The Doctor stood, went to the lamp, and studied the flowers. "It's a strange flower," he said. The Psychologist leaned forward to see, holding out his hand for a sample.

"It's a funny thing," said the Doctor. "I'm a good student of plants, but I have never in my life read of or seen this type of flower. May I have them?"

"Certainly not!" replied the Time Traveler.

"Where did you *really* get them?" asked the Doctor.

"They were put into my pocket by Weena when I traveled into future Time." He looked around the room. "But I'm very confused. This room, and you, and the things that have happened are too much for my mind. Did I ever make a Time Machine, or a model of a Time Machine? Or is it all only a dream? They say life is a dream, a very poor one at times, but I can't stand another dream that won't make sense. It's crazy. And where did the dream come from? I must look at that machine—if there is one!"

He picked up the lamp quickly and left through the door. We followed him into the workshop. There in the flickering light of the lamp was the machine—a thing of brass, ebony, ivory, and shining quartz crystal. I put out my hand and felt the rail of it. It was solid to the touch. There were brown spots and smears on the ivory, and bits of grass and green moss on the lower parts. One rail was crooked.

The Time Traveler put the lamp down on the bench and ran his hand along the bent rail. "It's all right now," he said. "The story I told you was true. I'm sorry to have brought you out here in the cold." He picked up the lamp, and, in complete silence, we returned the way we had come.

He came into the hall with us and helped the Editor on with his coat. The Doctor looked into his face and told him he was suffering from overwork. At this, the Time Traveler laughed loudly. I remember him standing in the open doorway, waving good-night.

CHAPTER EIGHTEEN

"Just Give Me Half an Hour…"

I lay awake most of the night thinking. I could not get the Time Traveler and his story off my mind. I decided to go the next day and see him again. I was told he was in the workshop and went to find him. The workshop, however, was empty. I stared for a minute at the Time Machine. Then I put out my hand and touched the lever. The thing swayed like a branch shaken by the wind. It startled me. (I remembered my childhood days when I had been told not to "meddle" with things.)

I came back through the hall and found the Time Traveler in the library. He had a small camera under one arm and a knapsack under the other.

He laughed when he saw me, and gave me an elbow to shake since his hands were full.

"I'm terribly busy," he said, "with that machine in there."

"But isn't it some trick or joke?" I said. "Do you really travel through time?"

"Really and truly I do." He looked into my eyes, then around the room. "Just give me half an hour," he said. "There are some magazines here you can read. If you'll stay for lunch I'll prove this time traveling to you, completely. I may even show you some pieces of evidence. If you'll forgive my leaving you now…"

I agreed, not knowing then the full meaning of his words. He nodded and went on down the hall. I heard the door of the workshop slam. I seated myself in a chair, and picked up a newspaper. What was he going to do before lunchtime? Then I remembered an appointment I had made with Richardson, the publisher, at two o'clock. I looked at my watch and saw that I could just about make it. I got up and went down the hall to tell the Time Traveler.

As I took hold of the handle of the door, I heard a shout, strangely cut short, and a click and a bang. A gust of air whirled around me as I opened the door, and from inside came the sound of broken glass falling on the floor. The Time Traveler was not there.

I seemed to see a ghostly, blurry figure sitting in a whirling mass of black and brass for a moment. It was so crystal clear that I could see right through it to the bench behind it. This phantom disappeared as I rubbed my eyes. The Time Machine had gone. Except for a stir of dust starting to settle, the far end of the workshop was empty. A pane of glass in the skylight had, I thought, just been blown in.

I was surprised and shocked at the same time. I knew that something strange had happened, but could not figure out what the strange thing might be. As I stood staring, the door to the garden opened, and the butler appeared.

We looked at each other. Then ideas began to come. "Has he gone out that way?" I asked.

"No, sir. No one has come out this way. I was expecting to find him here."

Then I understood. I stayed there, waiting for the Time Traveler, waiting for the second— perhaps still stranger—story, and the evidence and photographs he would bring back with him. But I am beginning now to fear that I must wait a lifetime. The Time Traveler disappeared three years ago. And, as everybody knows now, he has never returned.

One cannot help but wonder—will he ever return?

It may be that he swept back into the Stone Age among the hairy apes. Or into the early Jurassic Age among the reptiles.

It may be that he traveled into the future again and was caught up by the bloodthirsty Morlocks or the monstrous crabs. Or did he return to search for his little friend Weena among the pretty Eloi people?

To me, the future is still a blank, dark mystery, lit in just a few places by the memory of his story. And I keep next to me, for my comfort, two strange white flowers—shriveled now, brown and flat and brittle. They remind me that even when mind and strength had gone—somewhere in the future—thankfulness and tender friendship still lived on in the hearts of men and women.

THE END

H. G. WELLS

Herbert George Wells was born in 1866 in Bromley, Kent, England. His father was a shopkeeper and a professional cricket player. His mother had been a lady's maid.

When "Bertie" was a child, he broke his leg—and spent his recovery time reading book after book. Though he had to leave school at age thirteen to go to work, he won a scholarship to the Normal School of Science in London (a teacher's school) and studied under the famous biologist, Thomas H. Huxley.

Wells began writing articles and stories in 1893. When *The Time Machine* was published in 1895, Wells became an instant "hit" and he left his days of teaching behind. He published several "science fiction" works, including *The Island of Dr. Moreau* (1896), *The Invisible Man* (1897), and his most famous work, *The War of the Worlds* (1898).

Although Wells did not use the term "science fiction," he is known by many as the "Father of Science Fiction." (He had an ongoing rivalry with another science fiction writer of his day—Jules Verne.) H.G. Wells died in 1946.